Tyler's Pumpkin Patch.

Printed in the USA.

First Printing, 2015.

ISBN: 978-1508636250

Tyler's
Pumpkin Patch

Written by
Gene Brown

2015

Illustrated by
Anne Zimanski

To anyone who has ever had a dream and the courage to believe…

To my family, friends, teachers, and coaches –
you know who you are… you've all played such important roles
in my life - without you, I would've awoken from my dreams
years ago… for that, I am extremely grateful.

To my brother Tyler,
you inspire me to live strong every day - without you, this story
would literally not be possible.

To my parents, especially my mom –
who has always made me believe that I can truly do anything.
I'll love you both forever.

Tyler is what you would call a dreamer; a dreamer is someone who creates fantasies and worlds in his head. If someone read a story to Tyler about airplanes, he would go home and try to build his own airplane.

If Tyler saw a movie about pirates, he would cruise the ocean blue using the couch in his living room as his boat.

If Tyler dreamt it… you'd find him doing it.

It was fall. Fall is the time
of year when the weather gets colder and the
leaves on the trees start to change to beautiful colors like red,
yellow and brown.

As Tyler walked to school, the crisp wind blew the fallen leaves
around him and in his face. Tyler kicked through the leaves, imagining he was
a drummer marching in a band.

That day in school, Tyler's teacher Ms. Barden read the class a story about pumpkins.

"Pumpkins are orange and are popular during the fall months of October and November", said Ms. Barden. "They come in all different sizes, some are fat, some are tall, some are bumpy, and some are small."

"Can you eat pumpkins"? asked Tyler's classmate, Shannon.

"Ewwww!" cried all the children.

"Yes you can," answered Ms. Barden. "Pumpkins are in the squash family. There are many good foods made with pumpkin. There's pumpkin bread, pumpkin pie, and pumpkin soup."

"I love pumpkin pie!" said Corey.

"Me, too!" agreed the rest of the class.

"Where do pumpkins come from"? asked Tyler.

"Pumpkins grow in a pumpkin patch," answered Ms. Barden.
They sprout from a tiny seed that grows in the ground. When pumpkins are fully grown their insides are filled with seeds that you can eat. In fact, I have a surprise for you…" The children sat up straight with excitement.

Ms. Barden then pulled a bag out from behind her chair. The bag was filled with tiny white looking things.

"What is that"? asked Caylin curiously.

"These are actual pumpkin seeds that I brought in for you to try," said Ms. Barden. "Hold your hands out and I'll give you some."

"They're really chewy!" shouted Nicole.

"I think they're good!" said a few others.

Everyone was enjoying his or her pumpkin seeds, everyone, except for Tyler. He was sitting quietly with his head down, staring at the seeds in his hands. He had something else on his mind…

That night after supper Tyler went out and sat on his back porch. He opened the small bag that his teacher had given him. Inside were the five pumpkin seeds. Tyler ate a couple. "Not bad," he said aloud, "better than the broccoli we had tonight." Just then he heard his mother's voice calling from inside.

"Tyler, come clean up before bed!"

Tyler went to swallow the last of the pumpkin seeds in his mouth when he hesitated, thought for a moment, and then spit three seeds over the rail. He watched as the white seeds floated down, landed into the wet muddy grass, and disappeared.

Tyler stood staring into the mirror brushing his teeth. The mirror was still foggy from the hot bath he had just enjoyed. With one hand doing the brushing, he reached up with his other to the misty glass and outlined with his finger a giant round silhouette.

That night in bed, Tyler had a dream. But this wasn't an ordinary dream. No sports, no pirates, and definitely no airplanes. This dream was more real and more exciting than any other dream Tyler had ever had before.

When Tyler awoke to his mother calling him for his favorite breakfast, he jumped out of bed quicker than a cat from a tree and ran out of his bedroom.

He darted through the kitchen, past his Mom and Dad at the table, past the *Cinnamon Toast Crunch*, and out the back door.

Tyler ran down the back steps and into the back yard, his face wide with excitement. He looked everywhere, *around* the bush, *next* to the swing set, even *under* the picnic table… but there was nothing. His yard was exactly the same as the day before. Tyler's grinning face was quickly turning into a frown of disappointment.

"What's wrong Tyler?" asked his Mom standing behind him.

Silence.

"What is it?" said his Dad in a stern voice. Tyler turned around.

"Well, remember the pumpkin seeds I came home from school with yesterday?" His parents nodded. "When I was eating them last night on the porch I dropped three onto the grass, and last night I dreamt that a giant pumpkin patch grew in our back yard, pumpkins of all sizes, with dark green thick vines and big leaves… it was amazing!"

Tyler's parents looked at each other then back at him. "Tyler Honey, it was just a dream, pumpkins grow on a farm, not in back yards"… said his mother.

But they did grow!" shouted Tyler, "I saw them with my very own eyes… it was so real… I dreamt it!"

"Dreams are dreams, and are not real, Tyler", said his Dad. "I know you like to pretend and that you daydream a lot, but sometimes having too big a dream can end up hurting you."

"But… it was so real," cried Tyler again.

"I'm sorry little guy", said his father with an outstretched hand.

"C'mon, let's go eat breakfast and get you to school… maybe we can buy a pumpkin this afternoon. "

No one at school believed Tyler either; not even his closest group of friends. At recess, whenever he told them the story of the giant pumpkin patch in his back yard he dreamt about, they laughed.

"You're silly", said Andrew.

"That would never happen Tyler", said a voice through a group of giggles.

"We'll believe it when we see it!" shouted Nicole and Joey.

Tyler felt sad… very sad.

Fall left as soon as it had started and the seasons began changing. Winter came and Tyler's backyard was covered with frost and snow. Normally, Tyler loved the winter, the snowball fights, and the building of snow castles, but not this one - something he wanted was missing.

Months passed, the ice and frost began melting away from the branches and bushes. Tiny buds were sprouting on trees and flowers were popping their heads from the ground. The sweet smell of spring and life was in the air. The sound of children's voices could be heard throughout the neighborhood playing. Tyler's voice was one of them, but every afternoon when he got home, he'd go to his backyard.

Every hopeful glance quickly turned to disappointment… nothing; Tyler's backyard was the same as always. He was beginning to believe his dream would never happen.

Spring turned into summer and every tree on the street was filled with dark green leaves. The sun was strong and children who refused to put sun block on walked around with painful sunburns. Tyler was in his sandbox playing "buried treasure", a game very popular among the neighborhood kids.

It had been so long since he spit the seeds off his porch that he was starting to forget about them. ...Well, ALMOST. Before he went in, Tyler drew a giant pumpkin with his finger in the sand. Summer was almost over...

It was now mid September, one year had passed since the spitting of the seeds. Tyler remembered Ms. Barden telling the class that pumpkins usually grow during late September, early October. The day was now September 12th. "I still have some hope left," thought Tyler.

That night Tyler went to bed in his usual fashion. He took a warm bath, made sure to wash behind his ears, and brushed his teeth. He hugged his parents goodnight, grabbed his bear, and hopped into his big bed.

Nothing was out of the ordinary, however, that night Tyler fell asleep faster than normal. He was out as soon as his head hit the pillow.
Little did he know, what the morning would bring…

"Tyler… breakfast!" shouted his mom from a distance.

Tyler rolled over and rubbed the crusties from his eyes. He swung his legs down onto the floor and with his arms outstretched he let out a giant YAWN. His room was still totally black with only a little glimmer of the morning sunshine creeping through the cracks of his bedroom windows. Tyler, trying not to trip over his toys on the floor, walked toward the window to open the shade.

Yank, whip and SNAP! The shade flew up almost hitting Tyler on his nose. For a moment, Tyler's eyes adjusted to the strong sunlight, and then he looked out the window and into his backyard…
and that, is when he saw it…

"MOM, DAD!!!!" Tyler yelled at the top of his lungs. "COME HERE!!!"

Tyler's parents, thinking something was terribly wrong, made it up the stairs and into his room faster than a dog chasing a cat.

"What's wrong, Tyler? Is every thing okay??" asked his father out of breath.

"Look!"… Tyler pointed out the window.

"I don't believe it…" said Tyler's mother looking up at his Dad who was lost for words.

But it was true… outside through Tyler's window in his backyard; laid the biggest pumpkin patch anyone had ever seen. There were dozens of them with dark green vines tangled all throughout. There were fat ones, small, tall, lumpy, bumpy, and oddly shaped ones. Green pumpkins, greenish yellow pumpkins, and bright orange ones… there were so many!

Tyler's parents stood in silence, but Tyler stood with the biggest, whitest smile any little boy had ever had. He wasn't the slightest bit surprised. His dream had come true.

Over the next several weeks Tyler was not only the most famous kid in school, but in the whole town as well. A picture of him and his pumpkin patch could be found in every local newspaper and on the television news channel.

People came from all over just to see what such a little boy had done on his own. Lines of people would wrap around Tyler's house and expand down the street, seemingly going on forever. No one could be prouder than Tyler himself.

On one beautiful fall day, Tyler invited all the children and teachers from his whole school to his house to choose a pumpkin of their own. Everyone was there, the principal, the vice-principal, the janitors, and even Tyler's teacher Ms. Barden came.

Tyler's classmates, smiling widely, believed him now more than ever as they playfully looked around for a pumpkin. That very night everyone gathered at the school parking lot and carved a "Jack-O-Lantern". Every window in the whole school had a scary candle-lit face in it. It was spooky, yet one of the most beautiful sites anyone in the town had ever seen.

The large crowd around the school stood in awe at the spectacular image.

"It's magnificent", said Ms. Barden.

"It looks like a giant castle!" cried the children.

Everyone's eyes were glued on the school; everyone but Tyler... he had other new things on his mind...

The End

"No Dreamer is ever too small; No Dream is ever too big…"
-Unknown

About the author:

Gene Brown was born and raised in Manchester, NH.
He attended the University of Massachusetts Amherst where he graduated
in 2007. While substitute teaching kindergarten in the months following college
he was inspired to write a children's book after reading to one of his classes.

He still lives in his hometown of Manchester where he works as a sales
consultant for a medical device company. He enjoys working out, cooking, skiing
in the winter, and being outside with friends and family in the summer. He's
always working on making his dreams become a reality and always
will be.

You can visit him at www.tylerspumpkinpatch.com as well as ask questions and
interact with him personally at www.facebook.com/tylerspumpkinpatch.

About the illustrator:

Anne Zimanski is a Michigan based artist, with a degree in Illustration earned
from Kendall College of Art and Design in 2012. She knew from a young age
that she wanted to pursue art as a career, and never gave up that dream.

Today, Anne has illustrated dozens of books and works on a wide range of
projects with people from around the world. She is also an active volunteer
with local art groups, and teaches classes at a community art center. She loves
to spend time with family and friends, and relax on weekend trips to the Great
Lakes to enjoy the beautiful sunsets over the Saginaw Bay.

Her work and contact infromation can be found at www.annezimanski.com.

Author's note
A lesson idea for Teachers:

Read "Tyler's Pumpkin Patch" to your class during the fall months of September,
October, or November… or after a lesson about pumpkins and pumpkin
patches.

After the story is finished, distribute a small plastic baggy to each child
containing a handful of pumpkin seeds which they can take home with them.

That's it. It's that simple… Let their imaginations do the rest…

Made in the USA
Charleston, SC
05 March 2015